SPIRITED STEPHEN

and the
Healthy Hiccups

CAMECIA AKINLABI

To order additional copies of this book, contact:
Xlibris
844-714-8691
www.Xlibris.com
Orders@Xlibris.com

ISBN: Softcover   978-1-6698-4255-2
       EBook   978-1-6698-4256-9

Print information available on the last page

Rev. date: 08/24/2022

Dedication

As a child growing up in the south, we were always told hiccups were good for you because it meant you were growing.

Therefore, to all the Spirited Stephens out there, may life's hiccups help you to continue to grow.

~ "Let perseverance finish its work so that you may be mature and complete, not lacking anything."

James 1:4 NIV

Stephen was excited about his new project for science class, and he could not wait to get started.

Stephen's class was learning about different habitats that animals and plants live. He could create a model habitat of his choice.

Stephen thought to himself.

"I know that all the habitats are important to our environment, but I have just one little problem."

"Which one should I do?"

"I liked learning about all of them.

Stephen remembered something he had heard about feeling stuck on a problem.

When you come to a problem and you feel like it's holding you up, just remember it's only a healthy hiccup.

Stephen knew that healthy meant something good and a hiccup is a quick sound when you inhale. He also knew that a hiccup meant a small problem.

"I will figure out how to solve this problem."

Stephen thought for a while.

"Aha!

"I will make a list of habitats and write what I like about each one. Then I will choose the one I like most."

"Can't let this be a hang-up!"

"I just solved my healthy hiccup."

Stephen made his list of habitats.

"I got it, the tropical rainforest!"

"I like that it's hot, sunny, wet, a lot of different kinds of plants, animals and it is good for the environment."

Stephen started gathering materials he would need to make his rainforest project.

"Now what can I use to make it, so it will hold up?"

"Oh no, not another healthy hiccup!"

Just then, Stephen's little sister burst into his room.

"Hi Big Bro, don't mean to interrupt.

"Did I hear you say, healthy hiccup?"

Stephen thought to himself.

"Well, yes, Lil Sis."

"I need to make a model of a tropical rainforest."

"I don't know what to use to make it."

"No problem Big Bro, you're in luck. I can help with this healthy hiccup."

Stephen's little sister ran to the garage and gathered different size boxes.

"Look Big Bro, have at it, you choose!"

"Wow, Lil Sis, what a great roundup!"

"Thanks for helping with my healthy hiccup."

Stephen started on his project. He looked at rainforest pictures from books, magazines and the internet.

He drew and cut out different animals of the rainforest. He made trees and different plants.

Feeling okay about his project, Stephen stood back and looked at it.

He felt like something was missing.

"I need some trees to stretch up to the top of the box.

"Then I can add colorful birds, and other animals that make the tropical rainforest their home."

"Got it!"

"I'll add another box at the top."

"Can't let this hold me up."

"I've got this, healthy hiccup!"

Stephen worked some more on his project until he was finished and felt good about it.

"This looks great, if I say so myself."

Stephen's little sister came into his room.

"Amazing Big Bro!"

"Your project looks great!"

Stephen looked at her with a smirk on his face.

"Thanks Lil Sis, and with your help, I didn't give up."

"That's how to solve a HEALTHY HICCUP!"

Author Notes

Readers should understand and be able to share what they have read. This gives a reader an opportunity to validate their understanding, opinions, experiences and new learning. Sharing also helps with a readers' mindset.

At the end of the book is an *Author Share:*

- The first two sections are **"Word Share and Word Play"** that can help readers explore new words.

- The next section is **"Think Share"** that gives readers the opportunity to express their understanding, ideas, opinions and experiences .

- The last section is a **"Mindset Comic"** that will encourage readers to reflect on information they have read, to a related experience they have had by creating a comic strip of their experience.

Author Share

Word Share

environment- The surroundings of a person or animal in which they live.

habitat- The area where things live.

healthy- To be good for you.

hiccup- 1. A problem that stops you for a short time.

2. A quick sound made by inhaling.

interrupt- To be stop in the middle of an action.

project- A plan or design.

roundup- The gathering of things.

Word Play

*What do you call a *good problem*?*

Think Share

1. What is a *healthy hiccup*?

2. How does having a *healthy hiccup* make you feel?

3. What will you do if you get a *healthy hiccup*?

Mindset Comic

Create a mindset comic strip of a *healthy hiccup* you have had. What happen at the beginning, middle and end?

You Try!

~ "Let perseverance finish its' work, so that you may be mature and complete, not lacking anything."

James 1:4 NIV

Printed in the United States
by Baker & Taylor Publisher Services